Rascal

TRAPPED ON THE TRACKS

Collect all of Rascal's adventures:

Rascal

TRAPPED ON THE TRACKS

CHRIS COOPER

ILLUSTRATED BY JAMES DE LA RUE

EGMONT

EGMONT

We bring stories to life

First published in Great Britain in 2015
by Egmont UK Limited
The Yellow Building, 1 Nicholas Road, London W11 4AN

Text copyright © 2002 Chris Cooper
Illustration copyright © 2015 James de la Rue
The moral rights of the author and illustrator have been asserted

ISBN: 978 1 4052 7529 3

58625/1

www.egmont.co.uk

A CIP catalogue record for this title is available from the British Library

Typeset by Avon DataSet Ltd, Bidford on Avon, Warwickshire
Printed and bound in Great Britain by CPI Group

For Emma Madeline

CHAPTER 1

Steak! That's what Rascal had been thinking about when he saw the squirrel. A great big, fat, juicy steak . . .

It wasn't as if he'd always eaten like that in the old days, back when he still had a home. Just once, as a special treat,

his owner, Joel, had
given him steak
for dinner.

'Don't go
getting used
to this,' Joel had
laughed, and then he
had ruffled Rascal's ears. The memory
of that steak kept Rascal going now. He
could smell it. He could even imagine

the wonderful juices trickling down his chin as he bit into it.

There was just one problem. Here he was, out in the middle of nowhere. There was no Joel, there was no steak. Nothing but trees. It seemed as if he had been running through this forest all morning. He hadn't seen any other animals, but from time to time he'd been aware of unseen eyes watching him.

Once or twice he'd heard a rustle of leaves and caught sight of a pair of small back legs disappearing from view.

His hunger was like a ball of emptiness in his stomach. It just got bigger and bigger as the day slipped by. He sniffed at some berries on a bush. He'd seen the birds eating them, but he couldn't bring himself to taste one.

He'd have to get a bit more desperate before he started eating bird food!

That's when he spotted the squirrel. It was on the ground, holding an acorn in its paws and looking around primly. It didn't seem to have noticed him.

Rascal had never hunted an animal in his life, but now his hunting instincts kicked in. He charged forward. By the time the squirrel looked up, it was too late.

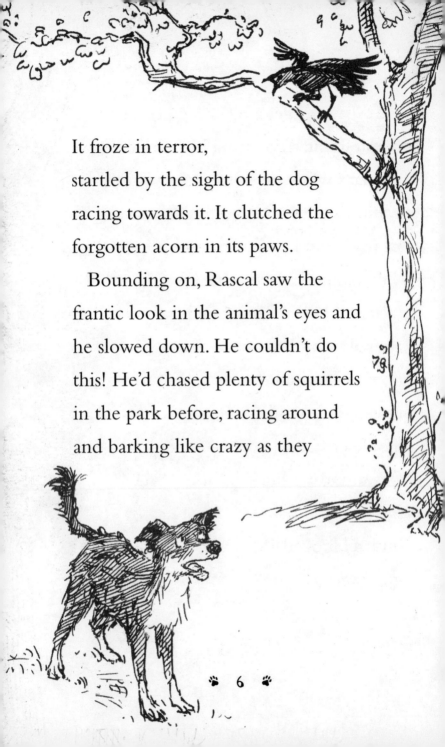

It froze in terror,
startled by the sight of the dog
racing towards it. It clutched the
forgotten acorn in its paws.

Bounding on, Rascal saw the
frantic look in the animal's eyes and
he slowed down. He couldn't do
this! He'd chased plenty of squirrels
in the park before, racing around
and barking like crazy as they

scuttled up into the trees. But that had been very different – that was only for fun. Chasing squirrels for food was another matter. He stopped.

The squirrel seized the opportunity. It snapped out of its frozen state and pelted up a nearby tree. Once it was high enough, it chattered angrily at the dog. 'Tchhrrrr!' Its voice was joined by the harsh cry of a crow in another tree. It almost seemed to be laughing at Rascal.

Rascal barked, although his heart

wasn't really in it. The crow didn't
budge, but the squirrel disappeared into
the branches. Rascal would have to find
something else to eat. But what?

He realised he was at the edge of the
forest. He poked his nose out warily.
It was good to see sky again. The
sun wasn't far from its highest point.
Rascal was glad to see it so that he

could be sure he was still going in the right direction. Home. As long as he kept going west . . . he knew it with a certainty that came from deep inside him. If he was ever to see Joel again, he had to keep on going west.

He paused and looked at what lay beyond the trees. Not much really – at least not much to a dog like Rascal, who had grown up in the city. Train tracks hugged the edge of the forest, separating the trees from a patchwork of neat fields. The fields stretched in front of him and at the far end of them sat a large house.

Rascal's ears pricked up with interest.

A house meant people, and people meant food . . . maybe. OK, it was too much to expect a steak dinner there, but he might be able to beg some scraps. It was worth a try. The ache in his legs told him that he couldn't go much further without food.

He stepped carefully over the train tracks, making sure he didn't get a paw stuck in the deep grooves between the metal rails. Then he ran down the embankment.

It was easy getting into the field through the fence. Rascal just flattened himself and crawled on his belly under the lowest bar.

He began to trot through the first
field. It felt good to be in the open air
again and just the chance of a decent
meal at journey's end gave him more
energy. A herd of cows huddled on
the far side of the field. They were
too interested in eating grass to notice
Rascal. Every so often one of them
let out a bored moo. Rascal couldn't

imagine living on a diet of grass — yuck!
Grass was for rolling in, not eating,
wasn't it?

He was halfway across the next field
when it happened. At first Rascal
thought that a bee had whizzed past
his ear. But then there was a sharp
CRACK!

Then another.

Something hit the ground near him –
something small and hard and *dangerous*.
A small cloud puffed up where the thing
had struck the dusty earth. The cows
were mooing in panic now.

Rascal looked around in alarm. There,
a long way across the field, was a man.
He was standing behind the open door
of a truck and holding a long stick-thing
to his shoulder. He was pointing it right
at Rascal.

The noise was loud even though the
man was so far away. Again something
small and fast zipped past him.

With a start, Rascal realised that he had to get away from here fast.

People were strange. Some of them – the good sort – didn't want to do anything but pat you on the head and give you bits of food. But others were dangerous. There was no time to wonder why this man was trying to hurt him. He could do only one thing – run!

But where? These fields offered no cover. Just moments earlier he had loved the feeling of being out in the open, but now he felt terribly exposed under the bright blue sky. The sun held him in its spotlight. *Here he is! Right here!* it seemed to cry.

Rascal turned and began to dash back towards the woods. In the distance behind him he heard a door slam and an engine rumble. The man had jumped into his pick-up truck. He was driving across the field. He was coming after Rascal!

Fear gave the dog extra speed. He put his head down and pelted for the woods. He forced himself not to look back at the truck, but he couldn't help hearing its rumble getting louder and louder. It was drawing closer.

But then suddenly Rascal became

aware of another noise. This was the
sound of an engine too, but it was
different. This one sounded somehow
bigger and more threatening than the
truck.

A horn roared its warning over the new rumble. As soon as he heard it, a memory came back to Rascal from when he was small. He knew what the noise was. A train! A train was coming!

What could he do? He had to cross the tracks and get away from the man with the gun.

CHAPTER 2

Rascal's legs ached and his heart was thudding. His chest burned as he gulped in more air and ran for his life.

The noise of the approaching train was so loud now that he could no longer hear the pick-up truck behind him. He glanced back and saw it zooming and bouncing across the field. It was close enough for him to see the man's face behind the wheel.

Suddenly, the train appeared round the bend in the tracks. It was enormous! It was fast too, and Rascal was afraid. Could he make it across the tracks in time and escape from the man with the gun? He put on a final sprint. His lungs felt as if they were about to burst. He bounded back up the embankment. The train had almost reached him. It was like a giant beast that would not stop for anything.

Rascal closed his eyes and flew across the tracks. The engine's din filled the air. Part of him was waiting for the giant train to smash into him, but the impact never came. He had beaten it . . . just!

As the mighty train rumbled by, Rascal tumbled down the embankment on the far side. He landed in an exhausted heap at the forest's edge and lay there panting. After a few moments, he looked up at the train. Rascal had only ever seen trains that humans would ride in to get from one place to another. But this was something else. It didn't seem to have any passengers in it. Instead there was boxcar after boxcar. They seemed to stretch back for ever. Some of them were full of stuff, while others looked empty. The clatter was deafening.

A terrible thought hit Rascal.

The train might look as if it went on for ever, but he knew that wasn't true. And when the train had passed, where would the man with the gun be? Perhaps he was on the other side of the tracks right now, patiently waiting for the freight train to pass?

Wearily Rascal hauled himself to his feet and plunged back into the forest.

Now he welcomed its cool darkness. At least there would be somewhere to hide in here. He ran on, no longer knowing or caring where he was going. His paws caught on tree roots, but whenever he stumbled he forced himself to carry on.

Then his nose began to twitch. Rascal slowed down at last. There was no mistaking that scent – there was a human in the woods too!

He padded into a clearing, making sure that he didn't step on any twigs that would give him away with a tell-tale SNAP! Suddenly he was staring into the face of a human.

But this wasn't the man with the gun. This person was younger, a girl. She was sitting on a fallen tree. She had a pad of paper on her lap and a pencil in one hand, but she wasn't using it. Instead she was just gazing at the sunlight slanting through the leaves. A jacket was on the ground by her feet. Its bright red colour seemed out of place in this world of green.

The girl looked up as he entered the clearing and their eyes met. Rascal was still tensed to run, but he relaxed a little when the girl smiled at him. There was a kindness in her eyes.

'Hello, boy,' said the girl. There was something soothing about her voice. Maybe this human was the good sort . . .

Rascal padded a little closer, still unsure. The girl put down her pencil and held one hand out. Her movements were slow and careful. 'Come here,' she said. 'You're a nice-looking doggie, aren't you? Are you lost?'

Rascal padded closer still. He understood the words 'come here', but the rest was a jumble of human noises to him. He was sure of one thing, however. This girl's voice was as gentle as the look in her eyes.

At last Rascal reached her. She moved her hand slowly so he wouldn't be startled. When her hand began to stroke the fur on the back of his neck, Rascal realised with a sudden rush how much he had missed the friendly touch of a human.

He tilted his head to one side eagerly. The girl took the hint and began to scratch his floppy ears. She got the right spot, just the way Joel always used to. Rascal snuggled closer to her, enjoying the feeling.

'You like that, don't you?' the girl laughed.

As she hugged him, Rascal closed his
eyes. He could almost imagine that the

last few days of
hunger and
loneliness
had been
nothing
more than a bad
dream. And now he was back where
he belonged – in the arms of a loving
owner.

A sound from the woods behind
him shattered the daydream. It was the
rustle of leaves, the urgent drumming of
footsteps coming this way. Rascal knew

what it was – the man with the gun. It had to be. After the train had passed, he must have decided to leave the truck behind and chase the dog into the forest on foot.

Rascal had to get away quickly! Panic and confusion swept through him.

The girl felt Rascal tense in her arms. 'What's wrong, boy?' she asked, puzzled. But by then the footsteps were loud enough even for human ears to detect.

The girl sensed the fear in the dog, but she didn't let go of him. Instead she kept one hand on his side and reached down to her jacket with the other. She lifted it up and whispered, 'Hide under here. OK?'

Rascal understood and he knew it was his only chance. The footsteps were too close for him to do anything else. He scrambled under the jacket and the girl quickly arranged it on top of him. The next thing he heard was the sound of someone bursting into the clearing.

CHAPTER 3

Darkness. It was warm under the girl's jacket, but Rascal couldn't stop trembling. He could feel the girl's leg pressing against him. Then there were human voices above him.

'What are you doing out here?' said a man.

Rascal stiffened with fear. It was the gruff sound of a voice that meant business.

The girl replied, 'I always come here. It's my favourite spot.'

There was a pause, then the man's voice softened a little. 'You've just moved into the old Armstrong place, haven't you?'

'We moved in a couple of months ago,' answered the girl. 'My name's Jenny.'

'Thought so,' said the man. 'Well, you're right, this is a nice spot, but I don't know that you should be coming out here on your own. See, there are coyotes and who knows what else. That's what I'm after now. I saw another coyote sniffing around on the farm. Might have been a wild dog. But whatever it was, you can bet it was up to no good. Might have been looking for calves – in broad daylight too. Have you seen anything?'

Hidden under the girl's jacket, Rascal felt the girl's leg press harder against him.

Her pulse quickened.

'No, I haven't seen a thing,' she said.

There was a long pause. And then Rascal heard the man speak again. 'Well, like I said, you should be heading home too. This is no place for you to be.'

'Thanks.'

Then it sounded as if the man walked away. Rascal didn't dare to poke his nose out to check. But after a couple of minutes, the girl called Jenny lifted the jacket from him.

Rascal sniffed the air. The scent of the man was fading and he could no longer hear footsteps. Perhaps he was safe now ...

Jenny took his head in her hands
and looked long and hard into his eyes.
Rascal looked back. He could tell that
she was making her mind up about him.
It was as if she was trying to look right
into his heart. At last she gave a brisk
nod and smiled.

'You don't care about silly old calves, do you, boy?'

Rascal wagged his tail and licked her face. Jenny laughed. Then she dug into her jacket pocket and pulled out a small packet of cookies. The smell coming from the open packet was so delicious it almost made Rascal do somersaults with excitement.

'Are you hungry?'

Those were words he could understand! The cookie was gone in exactly one second flat. Rascal hardly chewed it.

'Wow, that was a silly question! You must be starving!' said Jenny. She opened

her hands wide to show that there was no more where that came from.

'Sorry, all gone.' She studied Rascal a moment longer, then she jumped off the tree. 'But we'll soon fix that,' she said brightly. 'Come on, boy.'

Rascal hesitated for a moment. He knew that he liked this girl. And yet . . . did he dare to go back in the direction of the man with the gun?

Jenny seemed to understand his fears.

'Don't worry,' she said. 'We don't even need to cross the fields.'

Rascal hesitated for a moment longer. Finally it wasn't the thought of food that overcame his fear but the girl's kindness. He trotted after her.

'Good dog!' Jenny smiled, then she squinted at him. 'Only we need a better name than that . . .' She studied him and thought for a while. 'How about . . . Lucky?'

Seeing her smile, Rascal let out a bark.

'I'll take that as a yes. Lucky it is!' said Jenny.

They walked on further through the

woods. Rascal's worries about the man with the gun had begun to die down. He was just starting to relax when suddenly his nose told him that there was danger in the area. Dogs can sniff out enemies long before they see or hear them, and right now Rascal's nose was telling him that there was another dog nearby.

He froze, his hackles rising. Usually he wouldn't mind, but this wasn't just any old dog – not the kind you might run into in the park or anything. No, there was something wild and dangerous about this scent. There was something a little unnerving about it. Scary, even.

Jenny was looking back to see why he had stopped. She started to turn but stopped when she heard the low growl in Rascal's throat.

'Lucky, what's wrong, boy?'

But the dog wasn't growling at her. He was growling at whatever was hiding in the woods. He stared into a thicket of trees and felt sure that something in there was staring back at him. Rascal was afraid but he knew not to show it. He tried a bark, but nothing stirred in the forest.

'Come on, Lucky,' urged Jenny. 'We need to go now, if you want to get any food.'

Rascal took a final look into the tangle of forest. Then he turned and slowly trotted alongside Jenny. But with

every step, he could feel unseen eyes
burning into him from behind.

CHAPTER 4

The further they got from the woods,
the more Rascal relaxed. Every so often
he glanced round, but there seemed to
be nothing behind them now. He tried
to forget about it.

As they walked, Jenny talked and

talked. 'I like to come to the woods on my own most days, now that school's out. There isn't much else to do round here, I suppose, and I like to draw and just sit and think.'

The girl's words ran over Rascal like a stream of sound and he was content to let them. He was enjoying just walking and listening to Jenny so much that the shout took him by surprise.

'Hi there!'

Dog and girl both looked round with a start. There was a small lake off to one side of the road. A boy sat at the edge of the water with a fishing rod. He seemed

about the same age as Jenny.

'Hi,' mumbled Jenny.

She stared down at her feet and carried on. Rascal stood still, watching her walk on. Then he looked back at the boy, who was still gazing at them expectantly. Something in Rascal told him that this boy was a friend. The next instant, he bounded over to him.

'Lucky, come back!' yelled Jenny, but by then Rascal had already reached the boy. The basket next to him was a symphony of smells to the dog's sensitive nose – fishy smells, wormy smells, the deep, dark smell of soil.

'Nothin' here for you,' said the boy. He reached down and ruffled Rascal's fur. His touch was firmer than Jenny's. This was a boy who was used to handling animals.

He was friendly, but there was something familiar about him too. Rascal knew that he had never seen this boy before, and yet . . .

Jenny joined them. She looked
uncomfortable. 'Come on, Lucky,' she
insisted. 'We've got to get home.'

The boy squinted up at her. 'Nice-
looking dog,' he said. 'Is it yours?'

Rascal stared at Jenny. He could tell
that she was trying to decide whether

she could trust this boy or not. 'We're looking after him for a friend,' she said cautiously. 'His name's Lucky.'

'Probably ought to get a collar on him,' said the boy.

Jenny's cheeks flushed red. 'It's . . . His collar broke, but we're getting it fixed.' The more she spoke, the redder she seemed to get.

'It's Jenny, isn't it? You live at the old Armstrong place, right?'

Jenny nodded.

'I thought so. My name's Chris. So what brought your family out here, to the back of beyond?'

'My mum and dad got fed up with life in the city,' she said with a shrug. 'They felt it wasn't any kind of place for me to grow up in.' The words had the sound of ones she had given often in explanation. 'They thought I should have the chance to grow up in the country. You know, lots of fresh air, all of that.'

'You get a lot of that round here!' The boy laughed, then breathed in deeply and said, 'But make sure you stand upwind of the cattle shed before you enjoy all that fresh air.'

At last Jenny smiled. Rascal could tell she was relaxing a little. She pointed to the fishing rod. 'So have you caught any?' she asked.

'Couple of bluegills,' said the boy. 'Nothing worth keeping.' He looked back up at Jenny. 'Why, are you a fisher?'

She gave a little laugh. 'Never tried it.'

'Well then, have a seat and try your luck!'

Jenny hesitated. She glanced at the dog and said, 'No, I really ought to get Lucky home. He's hungry.'

Chris hid his disappointment. 'OK. Well, maybe some other time, huh?'

'Yes. I'd like that.' Jenny turned to go, with Rascal following at her heels.

Chris called out. 'Jenny, about your dog . . . while you have him here, I wouldn't take him for walks without his lead, if I were you. My dad's not so keen on dogs these days.'

Jenny froze. 'Who is your dad?' she asked.

'Tom Gilman. We own the farm west of your place.'

Rascal sensed Jenny's shy friendliness vanish in an instant. Chris noticed the change too. He furrowed his brow, and that's when Rascal realised who he must be. This was the son of the man with the gun! That's why the smell was so familiar. The boy's scent was similar. When he spoke, Rascal could hear echoes of his father's voice.

'Just be careful, OK?' said Chris.

'I will,' said Jenny flatly. Then she turned and walked away without another word.

CHAPTER 5

As they walked the rest of the way, Jenny's silence told Rascal that she was worried. And he knew why. It was because of the boy, Chris.

They had reached a small house by now. It was set a little way back from the road. Jenny led the dog to the driveway at the side.

'You stay here, Lucky,' she told him solemnly. 'I'll get you something to eat.'

Rascal knew the command 'Stay'. He immediately dropped and lay on the ground. He couldn't stop his tail from thumping against the dusty earth with excitement.

Jenny opened the door and disappeared inside the house. Rascal could hear the clatter of doors and drawers opening and closing. He fixed his attention on the door. It seemed like forever before it opened again.

But when it did . . . food! Jenny was carrying a plate which she set down in front of him.

'Lunch is served,' she said, grinning.

Rascal took that as an invitation to dive in. There were pieces of cold cooked chicken. OK, he could have

done without some of the vegetables
and other stuff with the meat, but that
didn't stop him from gobbling down
every bit of it. He was still licking the
last of the gravy when a new voice
spoke out from the doorway.

'What have you got there, Jenny?' It
was a man's voice. He sounded surprised
and a little confused.

'He was in the woods,' answered Jenny.
'Can I keep him, Dad?'

Rascal looked up to see a tall man. He
had a paintbrush in one hand and there
were paint splodges on his clothes. He
didn't answer Jenny's question. Instead

he called back into the house, 'Kate! Come and look at this!'

A moment later Jenny's mother was at the door too. She didn't need any explanation. One look at the way Jenny was ruffling the dog's fur told her everything.

'So can I keep him?' Jenny asked again.

Her mum folded her arms. Her voice was heavy

with sympathy. 'Oh, Jen, we don't know anything about him.'

'I know that he's clever,' said Jenny. She looked down into Rascal's eyes. 'Aren't you? Yes, you are!'

'His poor owner is probably looking for him right now,' her mum said.

Jenny pointed to Rascal's neck. 'I don't think so. I mean, he hasn't got a collar. And look at him – look how thin he is. I don't think he belongs to anybody. He's all alone, I'm sure he is.'

'He might be sick, hon. We can't take a risk like that.'

Suddenly the words began to tumble

from Jenny. 'I *know* he's OK. He's just tired and hungry, that's all. And if he was going to bite me or something, I bet he'd have done it by now!' The girl's eyes shone with tears. 'Isn't this why we moved out here anyway? To get away from the city and be in the open and all that? Well then, we should have a dog. We never had one before because you always said it wasn't fair to keep a dog in a little apartment . . .'

Jenny's voice trailed off. Her eyes were wet with tears. Her parents gave each other a long look. Her dad let out a sigh.

'Tell you what,' he said at last. 'I'm

making no promises, but he can stay tonight.'

'In the garden,' chipped in her mum.

'And in the morning,' continued her dad, 'I'll check if anyone's reported a missing dog in the area.'

'And if they haven't?' asked Jenny eagerly.

'We'll see,' said her dad.

'But you'd have to feed him and take him for walks,' added her mum.

'I will!'

'It's a big responsibility.'

'I know!' Jenny was beaming by now. When he saw the look on her face,

Rascal joined in with a couple of happy yelps. The girl bent down to him. 'I know what you'd like.'

She pulled open the garage door and began looking in the cardboard boxes in there. Soon she was holding something round and red in her hand.

'Hey, Lucky! Look what I've got!'

It was a Frisbee. To be honest, Rascal just wanted to rest his bones and have a nap, but there are times when dogs simply have to keep humans happy.

Actually, it was fun once they started playing. Jenny threw it and Rascal raced across the grass after the flying Frisbee.

He caught it before it hit the ground,
leaping up and plucking it out of the air
with his jaws. Then he carried it proudly
back to Jenny. Tired or not, Rascal
always enjoyed games like this.

The next time, Jenny threw the
Frisbee in the opposite direction. Rascal
charged off that way. He was halfway
across the lawn when he realised that the
Frisbee was nowhere in sight.

He looked back at Jenny. She was
grinning as she held it in her hand. She
hadn't thrown it at all.

'Wait for it!' she laughed.

Rascal barked his impatience. He had

come across this sort of thing before – it was one of Joel's favourite sneaky tricks too, when they played fetch in the back garden.

Jenny threw the Frisbee, for real this time. But Rascal didn't chase it. He just watched it floating away. He was thinking about his old master. What would Joel be doing now? How was he feeling? As far as Rascal knew, Joel thought that he was dead and gone.

'What's the matter, Lucky?' said Jenny. 'Go and get it!' She took a couple of steps as if she was going to fetch the Frisbee herself if he wouldn't. Rascal saw the happiness on her face. He barked once and charged after the Frisbee.

And then the telephone rang from inside the house.

CHAPTER 6

Jenny went on throwing the Frisbee and Rascal went on chasing it, but he was listening to the voice from inside the house as well. Jenny's mother had answered the telephone and the way she was speaking troubled Rascal. He could tell that something was wrong.

A couple of minutes later, Jenny's father came out of the house. Jenny and Rascal were playing tug-of-war with the Frisbee – another of Rascal's favourite games. Jenny's dad smiled when he saw the game, but there was sadness behind his smile. 'Jenny, your mum wants to talk to you,' he said quietly.

'OK, Dad.'

As she went into the house, Jenny's dad fixed Rascal with a level stare. He opened his hand and showed the dog the treasure hidden inside it – another cookie!

Rascal resisted the urge to leap up and pluck the cookie from the man's fingers there and then. He knew that wasn't the way you were supposed to handle these things. It wouldn't have done much good anyway. Jenny's father was a tall man and he was holding the cookie high in the air, up out of jumping range.

He walked towards the garage and opened one door with his free hand. Rascal followed, his eyes not moving from that cookie. When Jenny's father threw it into the garage, Rascal leapt after it like a cat pouncing on a mouse. He scooped it up from the concrete floor with his tongue. He was determined to enjoy the treat as much as possible this time, and so it probably took all of a second and a half to gulp this one down. It was only then, as the sunlight vanished, that he realised the garage door was shutting behind him.

'Sorry, boy,' he heard Jenny's father say. Then, from the other side of the closed door, 'It won't be for long.'

What was going on? Rascal wasn't sure, but he didn't like this. He liked it even less when he heard Jenny's voice from outside the garage. She had run out of the house and now she was shouting.

'But you said I could keep him! You said!'

'I know, but we just need to check it out. Mr Gilman said there was a wild dog on his farm this morning. He said some sheep have been killed a few miles south.' This was her mother, who must have followed Jenny outside.

'But Lucky wasn't doing anything on his stupid farm! I know he wasn't!'

'We just have to make sure,' said her dad.

'Things are different out here, Jen,' added her mum. 'These people make their living from animals. They can't afford to be —' But she didn't finish the sentence. Rascal heard the sound of crying and feet running. 'Jenny, come back!' cried her mum, but the only answer was the slam of a door.

Rascal listened to the silence outside the garage for a moment. Then Jenny's mother spoke quietly. 'What do you think?' she asked.

Her husband's voice also sounded

heavy with worry. 'I don't know,' he said. 'I just don't know. I mean, if a dog's had a taste of blood, then I don't think there's much we can do. We couldn't keep him.'

'We'll have to see what Mr Gilman says. He's coming over now.'

The voices became softer still. They were walking away from the garage, back towards the house.

'I know one thing,' said the man. 'Jenny's not going to take it well if we do have to get rid of the dog. A friend is what she really needs round here.'

Rascal heard the house door open

and close again. Of course, he couldn't understand everything they had discussed. He didn't need to. He could read the moods in their voices well enough. A tingle of anxiety grew within him. Whatever was happening, something told him that he would be better off away from this place he was trapped in. He had to get out of this garage.

But how? Rascal began to sniff around. The garage was full of boxes. Most of them were stacked up against one of the walls.

There didn't seem to be any way out, and yet there was the hint of a breeze in

the air. So where was it coming from? He found the answer when he sniffed around the back of the boxes.

In the far corner of the wooden garage part of a plank had rotted away. There was enough of a gap for Rascal to poke his snout through. He did so and then pushed and wriggled, hoping that his body would follow. It didn't. The wood dug into him as he pushed, but he didn't give up. If he pushed hard enough, perhaps the rotten plank would splinter and break further. He shoved with all his might, but it was no good. The gap was too small for him to squeeze through.

He pulled his head back and looked around for another way out. On the other side of the garage was a small window. It was set halfway up the wall and the only light in the garage came through its grimy glass. Perhaps he could get through there . . . if he could just run and make a jump for it . . . But Rascal knew that this was dangerous. He had learned the hard way that glass was something it was best to avoid.

But what else could he do? Nothing. He backed up as far as the boxes would allow him. He didn't have much room

to get up speed, but it would have to be
enough. He had tensed himself to run
when suddenly the garage door opened.

Rascal whirled round and found
himself looking into Jenny's face.

She held one finger to her lips.

'Quiet, Lucky,' she whispered. 'We're going to get you out of here.'

CHAPTER 7

Rascal followed the girl out of the garage. There was no sign of her parents. Loud music thumped from one of the upstairs windows of the house.

'They think I'm sulking and listening to music,' Jenny said softly. She gave him a grin, but it was more a look of determination than of happiness. 'Come on – this way.'

She led him to the road quickly, looking back at the house warily every couple of seconds. She relaxed – but only a little – when they were further down the road and a couple of trees blocked their view of the house.

'Mum was right,' she said bitterly as she looked down at the dog. 'People are different round here. That's why we can't wait for Mr Gilman to come with his gun.'

Rascal trotted silently beside her. They

passed the small lake where earlier that day they had seen the boy fishing. He was gone now. Jenny didn't say anything, but Rascal saw her brow crease with anger.

They carried on in silence and soon they were near the woods again. Rascal jumped up at her and licked her hand. He wanted to thank her for her

kindness. They would have to say goodbye here, before he crossed the train tracks and went back into the trees.

'Get down, Lucky,' the girl said. 'We've got a long way to go.'

It took a moment for Rascal to understand what she meant. Then he got it. The girl was leaving too! Of course! She had a rucksack on her back and it seemed to be packed full. Rascal's first reaction was one of joy – now he wouldn't be alone! There would be someone to play with him and look after him and keep him company . . .

But then he remembered the girl's

parents, the look of love in their eyes. She couldn't leave them behind. Rascal wouldn't allow it to happen.

He stopped and sat. Halfway up the embankment, Jenny turned and looked at him. 'What's wrong, Lucky?'

Rascal didn't budge, not even when Jenny walked back to him.

'Come on,' she said. 'We've got to

get moving.' Her voice cracked with emotion, but Rascal stayed put.

'Please,' she said through her tears. 'We won't be in time to catch the bus into town unless we go right now.'

Rascal returned her stare. What could he do now? If he stayed here, the man with the gun would surely find him. But he couldn't let Jenny run away from her home.

Suddenly he knew. It wasn't the nicest way to say goodbye, but there was nothing else for it. He gave a quick bark of farewell and began to run along this side of the embankment. Jenny couldn't possibly keep up with him.

'Lucky!' she shouted.

When he heard that cry, Rascal wanted to turn back, but he forced himself to keep on running. Jenny shouted again, but now her voice was further away.

He followed the bend in the train tracks, running as fast as he could. Suddenly his nostrils were filled with the wild scent he had smelled earlier. But this time Rascal did not sense unseen eyes drilling into him. Now the animal was standing right in front of him.

It was like no dog he had ever seen before. It was a coyote. Rascal had heard their howls only a few times in his life, always far away. Once he had even come across a faint scent trail in his old neighbourhood. But he had never seen one face to face like this.

The wild creature watched every move Rascal made. Then a snarl escaped from its jaws. Its whole body quivered as if ready to pounce. Rascal knew there was no backing down now.

Rascal looked into the coyote's eyes and in them he saw the wildness in his own heart. Every dog is two animals: there is the faithful companion and playmate of its master, but there is also the wolf inside the dog. In its secret heart, even the smallest of lapdogs will sometimes howl in the night and dream of the hunt.

Now Rascal let that wildness race through him. It was his only chance. He let out a bark and rushed forward. The coyote was bigger and heavier, and it was fast too. A lifetime of hunting for each and every meal had sharpened its reflexes. It reared up and came down snapping, hoping to get hold of Rascal's neck. Rascal ducked low and the coyote's jaws connected only with fur. But Rascal didn't stop there.

Putting his head down, he barrelled into the bigger animal, using his body as a ram.

The coyote was knocked off balance, but it remained on its feet. The two animals circled each other. Their eyes were locked together.

'Stop!' cried a scared voice from above him. It was Jenny! She had climbed the embankment and run along the train tracks to go faster and catch up. She was gripping a large stick in two hands, holding it in front of her like a weapon. Her eyes were big with fear, but there was bravery in them too.

At the sound of her voice, Rascal's eyes flickered away from his opponent's for just an instant. It was what the coyote had been waiting for. Suddenly everything was a blur of action. Rascal whirled back around and braced himself, but the coyote was not attacking. With a howl, it leapt past him and in the direction of the girl.

She waved the stick to defend herself, but the coyote wasn't attacking her either. It was fleeing, racing back to the cover of the woods. But Jenny didn't know that. As the coyote charged past her, she flailed wildly with the stick.

She took a step back and stumbled
on the loose gravel, falling backwards.
There was a thud as she hit the ground.
As soon as he heard that sound, Rascal
knew that it was bad.

He ran up the embankment to her.
Jenny didn't seem to be bleeding but she
was unconscious. She had hit her head
on one of the metal rails. Her eyes were
closed now, her breathing shallow. Rascal
began to lick at her face. There was
no response. He looked up to see the
coyote disappearing into the woods.

What now? His first thought was to
sit by her side – to guard her until she

woke up again. Yes, that's what he would do. Someone would come along to help, her parents perhaps . . . No, wait! He couldn't do that. Jenny was lying on the train tracks! What if a train came?

He tried to grip the back of her shirt with his teeth and pull, but he soon realised that this wouldn't work. Instead, he leaned his head against her side and pushed. She shifted a little, but not enough.

As he considered what to do next, Rascal saw the problem. One of Jenny's feet was wedged into the gap between two metal rails. Gently Rascal took the foot between his jaws and tugged. No luck. Then with his nose he tried to push her foot out of the shoe. Still no luck. Fear began to lap at his heart. What could he do?

A sound cut his thoughts short and the fear in his heart became a high tide of panic. The noise came from far away, but there was no mistaking it. It was the faint wail of a train's horn.

CHAPTER 8

Rascal knew what had to be done. He couldn't pull her free of the tracks, but a human would be able to. Jenny's parents! He had to go back to the girl's house.

Rascal whirled round and ran for all he was worth. His legs ached, but he ordered them on. He refused to slow down, because if he slowed down . . .

He was back on the road now. His paws scraped against the concrete surface. Past the fishing lake . . . no one there. His heart was pounding, his lungs screaming for him to stop and catch his breath, but Rascal ran on.

From a telegraph wire above the road,

a harsh cry sounded. It was the rasping
call of a crow. Again, it seemed to be
mocking the dog and what he was
trying to do. Rascal ignored it. He put
his head down and forced himself to go
faster still.

At last the little house was in sight,
but, as he got closer, Rascal realised
that someone else was at the house too.
Three people – adults – were standing in
front of the garage. Even from a distance,
Rascal knew who they were, because in
the driveway stood the pick-up truck –

the one owned by the man with the gun. A tremor of fear ran through Rascal, but Jenny's life depended on him. He didn't turn back.

When he got close enough to be heard above the wind, he began barking as loudly as he could. Jenny's parents and the farmer with the gun all turned to look his way. Rascal didn't realise it, but what they saw was a terrifying sight coming their way. He looked like a mad dog charging towards them.

The farmer, Tom Gilman, reached into the front of his truck and pulled out his rifle. He lifted it calmly to his shoulder. Rascal had left the road now. He was rushing across the front lawn, still barking with all his might.

The farmer put his eye up to the sight on the gun's barrel and moved his finger towards the trigger.

But suddenly another hand fell across the gun. It was Jenny's father. He said something to the other man and shook his head.

Rascal stopped barking for a moment, but he still jumped around frantically. He had to make them understand!

'What's wrong with him?' asked Jenny's mother. 'Do you think Jenny was with him?'

They all just continued to watch the dog. None of them made a move to do anything and Rascal realised that this was impossible. He could never make them understand, no matter how much he yelped and barked. There had to be another way.

Then he spotted it – the red jacket, the one that Jenny had hidden him under when they first met. It was still hanging where she had left it on the wooden fence.

Rascal ran up to it and took it in his teeth. He pulled the jacket off the fence

and began
to pelt back
towards the tracks.
He was dimly aware
of the shouts behind him, then
the roar of an engine jumping into
life. The humans were following – it was
all up to him now.

If the way to Jenny's house had been agony for the exhausted dog, now the way back to the tracks was a hundred times worse. But whenever he felt himself slowing, he remembered the brave look on Jenny's face as she had stood up to the coyote. Then he tightened his grip on the jacket and pressed on.

He could hear the rumble of the train ahead now. It sounded like a force of nature – like a storm, thunder and lightning. And it was getting louder!

At last Rascal reached the embankment. Jenny was lying on the tracks around the curve, but Rascal ran the other way, in the direction the train was coming from. He could see it now up ahead, an immense creature of steel racing towards him. Even though it was not yet dark, a headlight glared from the front of the train.

Rascal stopped running forward. He jumped as high as he could and began to wave the red jacket in his mouth from side to side. He felt small and foolish, and still the train continued to hurtle towards him. The blare of its horn was a hunter's roar now, a scream that told everything to get out of its way because

IT WOULD NOT STOP, IT WOULD NOT STOP!

The jacket fell from the dog's mouth.
It was too late. Nothing could help now.
And yet, amazingly, unbelievably, the
sound of the train changed.

Its eager rumble became a pained
screech. It was braking. The train was
trying to stop!

But a train like that doesn't stop easily. Time itself seemed to slow down as Rascal watched the huge vehicle pull up but nonetheless come closer and closer. Part of his brain told him that he should get off the tracks while he still could, but he didn't move.

At last the mighty train came to a stop. It was just metres away from the dog. Wearily, Rascal turned and ran back along the tracks to where Jenny was lying.

She had not moved at all and a dreadful fear clutched at Rascal's heart. But when he reached her, he could hear the girl's shallow breaths. He gave her face a lick and then took up guard beside her. He did not know how much time passed like that, but finally the girl's eyes fluttered open. She looked up weakly, trying to take in where she was and what was going on. Then her eyes focused and settled on the dog. A faint smile played on her lips.

'Lucky,' she said.

The dog was still sitting by her side when the train driver arrived. Not long after that came Jenny's parents and Mr Gilman.

As Jenny's dad carried her down the

embankment, the farmer speared Rascal with a glare. He said only one thing before striding away.

'Good dog.'

CHAPTER 9

Rascal was feeling fine. His belly was full and he'd spent the rest of the afternoon drifting in and out of sleep next to Jenny's comfy chair. He was half aware of everything going on around him. First there'd been the doctor. After examining Jenny, she had decided that the girl wouldn't need to spend the night in the hospital.

The next time Rascal woke, Jenny's parents had been talking to her.

'But why?' her mum had asked.

'I just wanted to see my old friends, that's all. I was going to call you once I got there.'

'But we can go and see your old friends any time. We'll take you. You know that. You just have to say the word.' This was her father.

'Really?'

'Of course!'

Then her mum, in a worried voice:
'But aren't you happy here?'

There was a pause before Jenny said,
'I sort of like it. But . . . it's a bit lonely
sometimes. Though now Lucky's
here . . .'

The rest of the conversation was lost
to him. It was as if his mind was falling

down a long tunnel into sleep and the voices above him were getting further and further away up at the top, until they disappeared altogether.

It was a deep and much-needed sleep. He woke up again only when Jenny's mum spoke.

'Jenny, there's someone here to see you.'

Rascal lifted his head. Jenny's mum was leaving the room and standing there at the door was Chris Gilman, the boy who had been fishing earlier that day. He looked embarrassed now. Unsure whether to sit or stand, he shifted from foot to foot.

'I . . . er . . . just wanted to see how you're feeling,' he said. 'OK, I hope.'

Jenny's eyes narrowed in sudden anger.

'Well, I don't want to see you!' she said. 'You told your dad about Lucky, didn't you? For all you cared, he might have killed him!'

Jenny was standing now. She turned and stomped off towards her bedroom. The boy didn't know what to do, but Rascal did. He didn't have long to act. He got up and stood in her way.

'Out of the way, please, Lucky,' said the girl. But for the second time that day

Rascal did not budge. It gave Chris a chance to speak.

'I didn't tell my dad anything,' he protested. 'He saw a dog on our land this morning and he started calling everyone in the area. And he wasn't coming round here to shoot anything. He just wanted to make sure your parents called the authorities.' His voice dropped. 'My dad, he gets a little crazy about coyotes and dogs sometimes, but he's just trying to keep the farm safe. When I was little, a wild dog came right into the yard. It didn't bite me or anything, but it turned out later that the poor thing had rabies.'

Chris stopped, waiting for Jenny to say something. She didn't until Rascal nudged her with his nose.

'So . . . what's that you've got in your hand?' she asked. She didn't say it outright until later, but there was an apology in her voice now.

Chris gave a sheepish grin as he showed her the card game he held.

'Well, I didn't think you could go fishing right now, but I thought you might want to play a game of Go Fish.' He blushed. 'You know, if you're bored or something.'

Jenny flashed a grin. 'Have a seat and

try your luck!'

Rascal stuck around for a while. It was nice to hear the two of them laughing and playing together. So nice that Rascal could almost imagine spending all his evenings here doing this. But he knew now that he could not. This was a nice home, but it wasn't *his* home. It would be best to hit the road while there was still enough light.

He padded silently to the door and took one last look at Jenny.

'Cheater!' she laughed, pointing at the cards.

'I am not!' spluttered Chris with jokey

indignation.

Jenny rolled up the sleeves of her pyjamas. 'OK then. From now on it's no more Ms Nice Girl . . .'

And at that moment Rascal knew that she would be fine. When he'd first seen her, he'd been struck by how lonely she appeared. Now, laughing and joking with her new friend, she seemed like a different person.

Rascal went into the hallway and lifted a paw to the front door.

'You want to go outside, Lucky?' asked Jenny's dad from the kitchen. He came and opened the door. Rascal trotted

outside and ran across the lawn. He
looked back at the small house.

Standing at the doorway to let the
dog back inside, Jenny's father suddenly
realised that the dog would not be
coming in again. He lifted one hand in
farewell. 'Live up to your name,' he said
quietly. 'Be lucky.'

CHAPTER 10

Rascal felt strong and full of energy now. He made good time, maintaining a steady trot that he knew he could hold for several hours to come. The sun was beginning to slide over the horizon when he reached the woodlands spreading westward.

Once again he plunged into the tangled shade of the forest. He had been going through the woods for quite a while when he saw something lying on the ground ahead. The thick hair at the back of his neck stood on end. It was the coyote again, the same one. There was no mistaking that scent. Would Rascal have to fight again?

But there was something wrong. The coyote wasn't moving. It was completely still. It couldn't be sleeping, not out in the open like that. Could it be . . .

A crow in a nearby tree had the same idea.

It let out a
hungry caw and flew
down to the ground. It
reached the coyote in a couple
of hops.

Rascal looked away, not wanting to
see what the bird did. But suddenly
there was a blur of motion. The coyote
leapt up, twisting its head round and

snapping at the crow. It almost got the bird, but the crow just managed to flap to safety. It did so with a raucously angry cry and an explosion of feathers.

The coyote did not seem bothered that its plan had not worked. It took its time standing up, now that the need for speed had gone along with the crow. The coyote was clearly aware that Rascal was watching, but it took a while to meet the dog's gaze. Its look was more curious than anything now, but Rascal's legs were tensed, ready to run or fight.

The coyote did not attack. Instead it put its head back and let out a howl.

'Owoooooooo!'

Rascal didn't know if it was a greeting or a warning signal, but one thing was certain – it was not an attack sound.

Seconds later a chorus of howls came in answer. These were higher-pitched and they didn't come from too far away. In an instant Rascal understood. These were the coyote's pups. The wild animal was intent on feeding its family. When it had fought Rascal at the tracks, it had been trying to protect its family too.

Rascal lowered his head and flattened his tail to show that he meant no harm. The two dogs – one wild, one tame –

held each other's gaze for a moment longer and then Rascal plunged on into the woods, making sure he looped around the coyote family in a wide circle.

He was still running when the sun had gone down and night had fallen. The moon was close to full, but Rascal didn't see much of it through the overhanging trees. Now the forest was home to a different set of animals – all the creatures that preferred to sleep through the sunlight hours and feed by night.

Not Rascal. It had been a long evening and he was ready to sleep. With his front paws he dug a shallow pit in the soil. It took a while to settle into it and get comfortable, but finally it was good enough. There was a noise in the distance. It was the far-off sound of the coyotes, miles behind him now. On the few occasions in his life that he'd heard coyotes howling before, they had always sounded strangely lonely to him. But tonight, though he lay alone, there was something comforting about hearing those howls in the dark. Rascal closed his eyes and let them lull him off.

In the grey area between waking and sleep, a face swam up to meet him. It was his master, Joel, smiling and calling his name. Even if only in Rascal's dreams, the two were together again. For now, that would have to do.

Rascal wants to get home to his best
friend Joel, but he's got a long way to go.
What will his next adventure be?
Find out in this special extract from

RUNNiNG FOR HiS LiFE ...

CHAPTER 1

It wasn't the noise of passing traffic that woke Rascal. It wasn't the brightness of the morning sun either, as it peeked out from behind the clouds, or the breeze that rustled the leaves of the bushes around him.

No, it was better than that. It was
the smell of sausages. That and the
wonderful sizzle they made as they
cooked. To Rascal's ears it was one of
the best sounds in the world. It seemed
to whisper, 'Come and eat us, come and
eat us! What are you waiting for?' When
a dog is as hungry as Rascal was, he
doesn't need a second invitation.

The sun was already quite high.
Rascal had slept long after sunrise. He
had arrived in this town late the night
before. He was weak and exhausted
and there was a little blood between
the pads of one of his front paws. He

had just wanted to slump in the nearest doorway and sleep, but he knew that he couldn't do that. He'd tried that once before, a few towns back, and an angry shopkeeper had shooed him away first thing in the morning. It wasn't the greatest way to wake up. Rascal knew now that he had to find a better hiding place before he could allow the blackness of sleep to fold itself around him.

So, when all he'd wanted to do was curl up and close his eyes, the dog had forced himself to pad around this strange new town in search of a safe place. There

was a small park near the square.
Rascal had found a clump of bushes
there and dug his way inside them. It
wasn't very comfortable and it wasn't
very warm, but that didn't stop Rascal
from falling into a long dreamless sleep
almost immediately.

The next thing he knew, it was
morning and . . . that wonderful smell of
sausages!